Pet of a Pet

by **MARSHA HAYLES**
illustrations by **SCOTT NASH**

Dial Books for Young Readers
New York

To Hannah, Lily and Nate—best of the best kids!
M. H.

For Nancy and Tip
S. N.

Published by Dial Books for Young Readers
A division of Penguin Putnam Inc.
345 Hudson Street
New York, New York 10014

Designed by Kimi Weart
Text set in Jacoby Light
Printed in Hong Kong on acid-free paper
1 3 5 7 9 10 8 6 4 2

Library of Congress Cataloging-in-Publication Data
Hayles, Marsha.
Pet of a pet/by Marsha Hayles; illustrations by Scott Nash.—1st ed.
p. cm.
Summary: Each of the farm animals takes another as a pet
and tries to impart to that animal his own characteristics or behavior.
ISBN 0-8037-2512-4
[1. Domestic animals—Fiction. 2. Pets—Fiction.
3. Identity—Fiction.] I. Nash, Scott, date, ill. II. Title.
PZ7.H3148895Pe 2001
[E]—dc21 99-20201 CIP

The illustrations were created using gouache and pencil.

Tabitha lived on a farm
with many pets.

Tabby, as she liked to be called,
had a pet horse named Brian.
Brian loved to nuzzle up to Tabby.

"You are such a smart horse,"
   Tabby said to Brian.
"I am going to teach you a trick."
   But *what* trick?

Tabby liked math very much.

"I know. I will teach Brian to add."

Brian worked hard.

"What is one plus two?" asked Tabby.

Brian lifted his brown hoof.

He stomped it three times in the dirt.

Clomp! Clomp! Clump!

"Smart horse!" Tabby cheered.

"Yippity ya-hoo! Best horse on the whole farm."

A certain cow agreed.

Brian the horse had a pet cow.
He named the cow Whinny.
Whinny fluttered her long lashes
whenever Brian was nearby.

"You are such a talented cow,"
Brian neighed to Whinny.
"I am going to teach you a trick."
But *what* trick?

Brian liked to run very fast.

"I know. I will teach Whinny to race."

Gal-lump! Gal-lump! Gal-lomp!

Whinny ran 'round and 'round.

"Talented cow!" Brian whinnied.

"Yippity ya-hoo! Best cow in the whole town."

A certain pig agreed.

Whinny the cow had a pet pig.
She named the pig Clover.
Clover loved to sniff the ground
Whinny walked on.

"You are such an amazing pig,"
Whinny said, to butter up Clover.
"I am going to teach you a trick."
But *what* trick?

Whinny loved to swish her tail.

"I know. I will teach Clover to swat flies."

Clover could not swish or swat.

But he could wiggle his curly tail.

Wiggle-waggle! Wiggle-waggle!

All the flies flew away.

"Amazing pig!" Whinny mooed.

"Yippity ya-hoo! Best pig in the whole county."

A certain rooster agreed.

Clover the pig had a pet rooster.

He named the rooster Oink.

Oink strutted proudly around Clover.

"You are such a brilliant rooster,"
Clover squealed to Oink.
"I am going to teach you a trick."
But *what* trick?

Clover liked to roll in the mud.

"I know. I will teach Oink

to flop down in the cool mud."

Oink flopped and he rolled.

Then he shook his feathers.

Shake, ruffle, and roll! Shake, ruffle, and roll!

"Brilliant rooster!" Clover snorted.

"Yippity ya-hoo! Best rooster in the whole state."

A certain dog agreed.

Oink the rooster had a pet dog.
He named the dog Doodle.
Doodle licked and licked Oink
with his floppy pink tongue.

"You are such a delightful dog,"
Oink crowed to Doodle.
"I am going to teach you a trick."
But *what* trick?

Oink liked to get up early.
"I will teach Doodle
to crow at sunrise."
Doodle could not crow.
But he could bark and howl.
Ruff-a-roo! Ruff-a-ro-o-o!
Every morning
Doodle woke up the whole house.
"Delightful dog!" Oink cackled.
"Yippity ya-hoo! Best dog in the whole country."
A certain cat agreed.

Doodle the dog had a pet cat.

He named the cat Rover.

Rover purred and purred

whenever Doodle was near.

"You are such a clever cat,"
Doodle barked to Rover.
"I am going to teach you a trick."
But *what* trick?

Doodle loved to pick up things
and bring them back.
"I know. I will teach Rover to fetch sticks."
Ska-daddle, nab, drop! Ska-daddle, nab, drop!
Rover fetched and fetched
until every stick on the farm
was in one huge pile.
"Clever cat!" woofed Doodle.
"Yippity ya-hoo! Best cat on the whole continent."
A certain someone agreed.

Rover the cat had a pet girl.

She named the girl Tabby.

Tabby loved to stroke Rover's soft fur.

"You are such a purr-fect girl,"

Rover mewed to Tabby.

"I am going to teach you a trick."

But *what* trick?

Rover loved to explore.

"I am going to teach Tabby

how to climb a tall tree."

Tabby learned quickly.

She and Rover climbed together.

Scootch, grab, upsy-up! Scootch, grab, upsy-up!

"Purr-fect girl!" Rover meowed.

"Yippity ya-hoo! Best girl in the whole world."

And from atop that tree, the two pets

could see the whole farm.

"Hmmm . . . silly pets!" said Tabby.

"Yep, the silliest!" agreed Rover.

Together they called:

"Yippity ya-hoo! Best farm in the whole universe!"

And who wouldn't agree?